W9-BGO-358

# Gaston

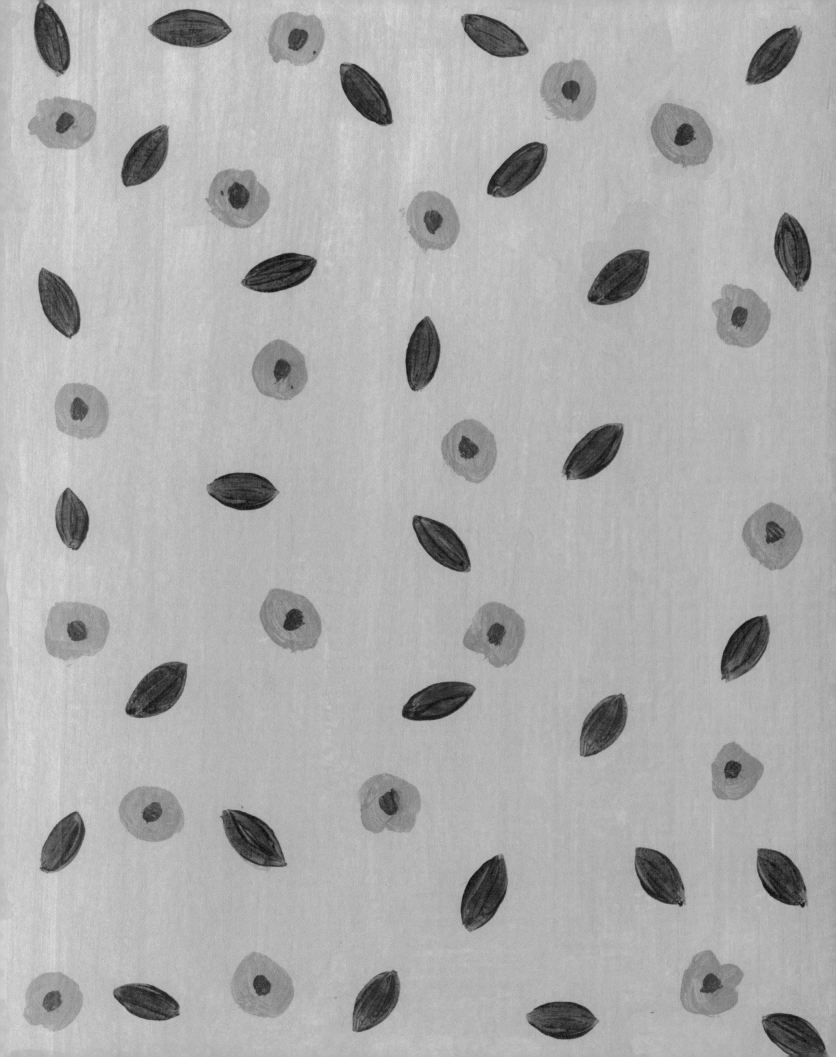

*For my
brothers,
Ronnie and
Michael
—K. D.*

*To my
high school
art teacher,
Ms. Kim
—C. R.*

No part of this publication may be reproduced, stored in a retrieval system, or transmitted in any form or by any means, electronic, mechanical, photocopying, recording, or otherwise, without written permission of the publisher. For information regarding permission, write to Atheneum Books for Young Readers, an imprint of Simon & Schuster Children's Publishing Division, 1230 Avenue of the Americas, New York, NY 10020.

ISBN 978-1-338-08900-4

Text copyright © 2014 by Kelly DiPucchio. Illustrations copyright © 2014 by Christian Robinson.
All rights reserved. Published by Scholastic Inc., 557 Broadway, New York, NY 10012, by arrangement with Atheneum Books for Young Readers, an imprint of Simon & Schuster Children's Publishing Division. SCHOLASTIC and associated logos are trademarks and/or registered trademarks of Scholastic Inc.

The publisher does not have any control over and does not assume any responsibility for author or third-party websites or their content.

12 11 10 9 8 7 6 5 4 3 2 1          16 17 18 19 20 21

Printed in the U.S.A.                          08

This edition first printing, January 2016

Interior design by Ann Bobco
Cover design by Christian Robinson and Ann Bobco
The text for this book is set in Adobe Caslon Pro.
The illustrations for this book are rendered in acrylic paint.

# Gaston

WORDS BY KELLY DiPUCCHIO

PICTURES BY CHRISTIAN ROBINSON

SCHOLASTIC INC.

Mrs. Poodle admired her new puppies.

*Fi-Fi*,   *Foo-Foo*,   *Ooh-La-La*,   and *Gaston*.

Would you like to see them again?

**Fi-Fi,**

**Foo-Foo,**

**Ooh-La-La,**

and **Gaston.**

Perfectly precious, aren't they?

Mrs. Poodle
thought so too.
The puppies grew
(as puppies do).
Three were no bigger
than teacups.

The fourth, however, continued to grow.
And grow. Until he was the size of a *teapot*.

Mrs. Poodle took pride in teaching her puppies how to be proper pooches. They were taught to sip. *Never slobber!*

"Good."

"Well done."

"Very nice."

"Nice try."

They were taught to yip. *Never yap!*

Yip. Yip. Yip.

RUFF!

And they were taught to walk with grace. *Never race!*

**Tip.** **Toe.** **Tippy-toe.**

WHOA!

The puppies were also taught
how to look pretty in pink,
nibble their kibble,
and ride in style.

Whatever the lesson, **Gaston**
always worked the hardest,
practiced the longest,
and smiled the biggest.

Mrs. Poodle was very pleased
with all her puppies,

Foo-Foo, Ooh-La-La,

Fi-Fi, and Gaston.

Spring arrived, and the proud mother was
eager to show off her darlings. She took them
to the park for their very first stroll in public.

There was much to see. Daffodils. Ducklings. Dogs.

Whatever the lesson, **Gaston**
always worked the hardest,
practiced the longest,
and smiled the biggest.

Mrs. Poodle was very pleased
with all her puppies,

**Foo-Foo**,   **Ooh-La-La**,

**Fi-Fi**,   and **Gaston**.

Spring arrived, and the proud mother was
eager to show off her darlings. She took them
to the park for their very first stroll in public.

There was much to see. Daffodils. Ducklings. Dogs.

Oh dear.
Who do we have here?

RICKY,

ROCKY,

BRUNO,

and
ANTOINETTE.

Would you like to see them again?

ROCKY,

RICKY,

BRUNO,

and **ANTOINETTE**.

This was more than a little awkward.
The mothers sized up the pups.
The pups sized up one another.

"It seems there's been a terrible mistake,"
Mrs. Bulldog said, breaking the silence.

*"Oui, oui,"* Mrs. Poodle agreed sadly. "Whatever shall we do?"
Mrs. Bulldog could not come up with an answer.
"I guess we'll let them decide," she replied at last.

**Gaston** and **ANTOINETTE** were young, but even they could see that there had been a mix-up. The two puppies began to circle around and around the group.

Gaston walked with grace.
ANTOINETTE raced.
Gaston yipped.
ANTOINETTE yapped.

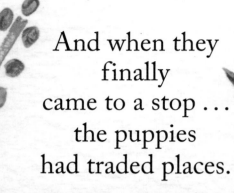

And when they finally came to a stop ... the puppies had traded places.

There.
That *looked* right ...

it just didn't
*feel* right.

That evening **ANTOINETTE** tried to fit in
with her new sisters, but she did not like
anything proper or precious or pink.

PHOOEY!

On the other side of town, **Gaston** tried to fit in with his new brothers, but he did not like anything brutish or brawny or brown.

*Ick!*

**ANTOINETTE** and *Gaston* weren't the only ones

who were having a hard time adjusting.

The next morning Mrs. Poodle forgot
all about being proper and raced
back to the park.

Mrs. Bulldog was already there waiting with her burly brood.

"It seems *we've* made a terrible mistake!" she nearly shouted.

*"Oui, oui!"* Mrs. Poodle agreed happily.

This time **Gaston** and **ANTOINETTE**
wasted no time trading places.

There.
That looked right.
And it felt right, too.

From that day forward the families met
in the park every afternoon to play.

**ROCKY, RICKY, BRUNO,** and **ANTOINETTE**
taught the poodle puppies a thing or two about being tough.

Likewise, **Fi-Fi**, **Foo-Foo**, **Ooh-La-La**, and **Gaston** taught the bulldog puppies a thing or two about being tender.

And many years later, when **Gaston** and **ANTOINETTE**
fell in love and had puppies of their own,
they taught them to be whatever they wanted to be.

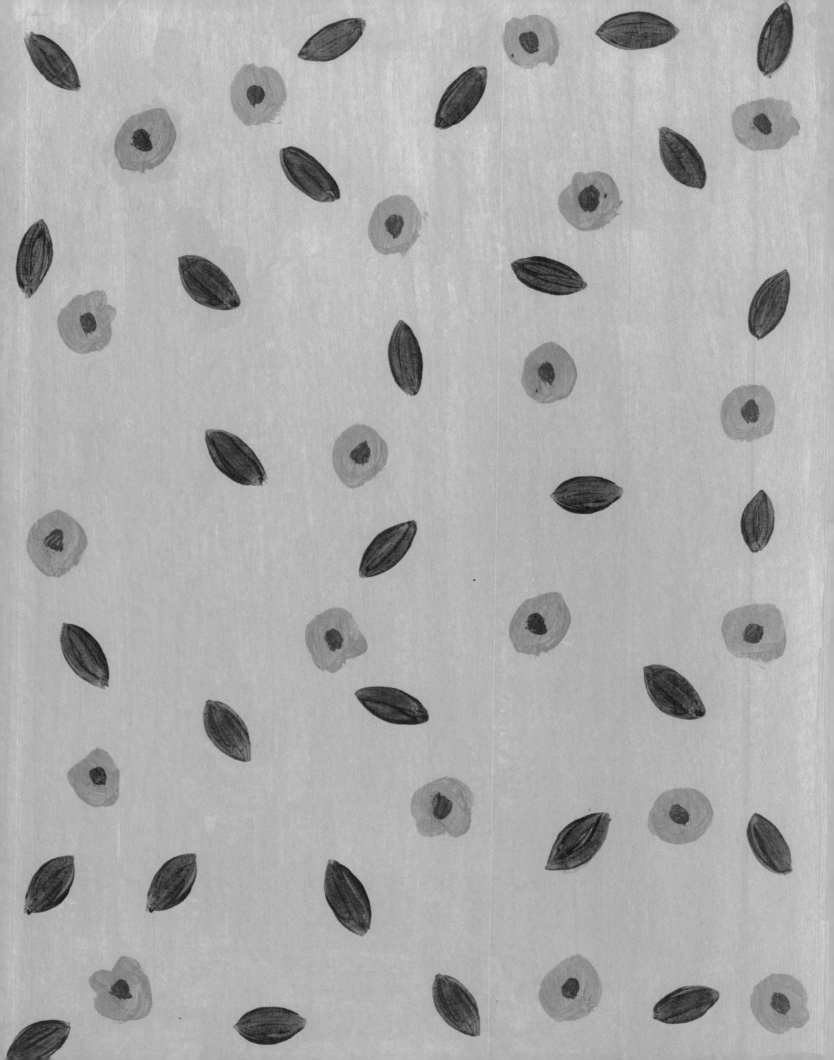

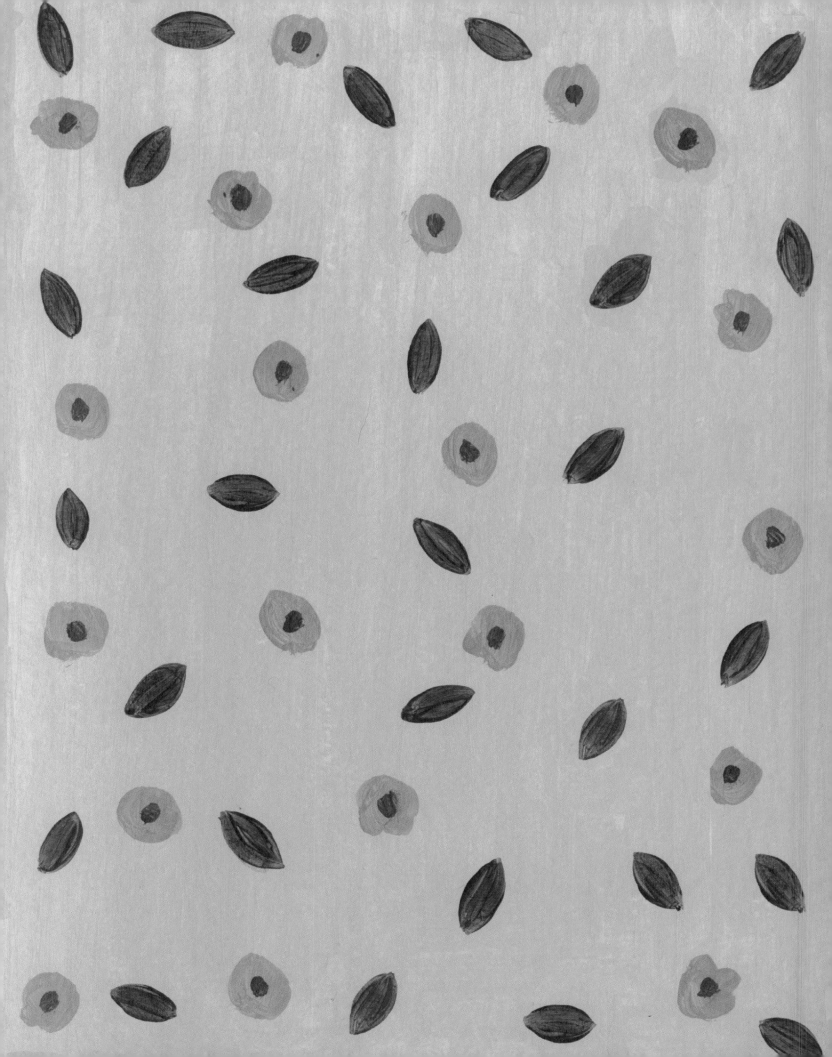